Cary Fagan

WOLFIE & FLY

Illustrated by
Zoe Si

TUNDRA BOOKS

Tundra Books, a division of Random House of Canada Limited,
a Penguin Random House Company

Library and Archives Canada Cataloguing in Publication
Fagan, Cary, author
Wolfie and Fly / Cary Fagan ; illustrated by Zoe Si.
(Wolfie and Fly ; 1)
Issued in print and electronic formats.
ISBN 978-1-101-91820-3 (hardback).—978-1-101-91821-0 (epub)
I. Si, Zoe, illustrator II. Title.
PS8561.A375W65 2017   jC813'.54   C2016-900962-9
                                                 C2016-900963-7

Published simultaneously in the United States of America by
Tundra Books of Northern New York, a division of Random House
of Canada Limited, a Penguin Random House Company

Library of Congress Control Number: 2016933013

Edited by Samantha Swenson
Designed by Scott Richardson
The artwork in this book was rendered in ink and watercolor.
The text was set in Fournier.
Printed and bound in the United States of America

www.penguinrandomhouse.ca

1 2 3 4 5   20 19 18 17 16

TUNDRA BOOKS | Penguin Random House

To my friend Anisha Neron
—CF

For Mom, Dad and Eevee—
my first and biggest fans
—ZS

CHAPTER I

Thanks, but No Thanks

Renata Wolfman wore the same thing every day. She wore a white T-shirt, overalls and sneakers. She *never* wore anything else.

One Saturday morning, her mom asked, "Renata, how about going clothes shopping today?"

"Thanks, but no thanks," Renata answered. She was curled up in a comfy chair, reading a book on sea turtles.

"Wouldn't you like something different to wear for a change? Something pretty?"

"Not particularly."

"Hey," said her dad. "Why don't we all go shopping? You can buy whatever clothes you want."

"Whatever I want?"

"That's right."

"Okay," Renata said. So she went shopping with her parents and bought three new white T-shirts and two new pairs of overalls. She put them away in her closet and picked up her book on sea turtles again.

Sea turtles, she thought, were a lot more interesting than clothes.

Renata didn't have any friends.

Not even one.

Did this bother her? No, it did not. Renata didn't want any friends. She thought that other kids were annoying. Other kids whined or talked too much or told stupid jokes or wanted to play boring games. Other kids weren't interested in the same things as Renata. They just got in the way.

Friends? thought Renata. Phooey!

"But everybody needs friends," said her mom on the following Saturday.

"Not me," Renata said. She didn't

bother to look up from the book on sharks she was reading. She crunched on some dry cereal. She drank some milk from her glass. Renata liked to keep things separate.

"It isn't healthy to have no friends," her mom insisted.

"I'm perfectly healthy," Renata said. "Friends have germs. Their noses drip. They cough all over you. I'm *much* healthier without them."

"I have an idea," said her dad. "How about inviting over that nice boy from next door. What's his name?"

"Livingston," said her mom. "Livingston Flott. I think that's an excellent idea. What do you say, Renata?"

"We don't have anything in common," Renata said.

"You're both human beings," said her mom. "And his parents say he's very smart. And creative."

Renata groaned. "Creative people like to make things up. I prefer real things. I prefer facts."

"I know you do," her dad said. "But it would be nice to invite Livingston over. I don't think he has many friends, either. Renata, are you even listening?"

"Ocean life is just so fascinating," Renata said, turning the page of her book.

Her parents gave up. They went off to discuss new wallpaper or whatever it was parents did in their spare time.

Renata smiled. Once again she had gotten her way.

🐟 🐟
🐟

On the next Saturday afternoon, her mom said, "Let's go, Renata. We don't want to be late."

"Late for what?" Renata asked. She was examining one of her sneakers. She wondered if it would be possible to make your own sneakers. Out of duct tape, maybe? Duct tape was good for just about anything.

"Don't tell me you've forgotten. Today is Uncle Bob's retirement party. He finished his very last day of work at the Perfecto Toaster Company."

"Your uncle is going to barbecue steaks," said her father.

"I don't eat meat," Renata said.

"Since when?" asked her mom.

"Since this morning. I read a book on being a vegetarian."

"Then you can have toast," her dad said. "Uncle Bob has every model of toaster the company makes."

"I'm kind of busy," Renata said.

"Sometimes," her dad said, "you just have to do what you're told."

"Thanks, but no thanks."

"Do you hear your father?" said her mom. "You're coming and that's an order."

Her parents left without her.

Renata nodded with satisfaction. She had the house all to herself, just as she liked. The question was what to do first.

CHAPTER 2

Bigger

Renata liked to make things.

She was good at it. And she liked making them all by herself. That way she didn't have to "cooperate" with others, the way adults always insisted. She didn't have to "compromise" or "respect other people's opinions." She could do things just the way she wanted.

"I like my own opinions, thank you very much," she said out loud.

In her room was the model of the Golden Gate Bridge that she had made out of Popsicle sticks. It had taken three hundred and twelve sticks and four bottles of glue.

In the bathroom was her model rainforest. She had stuck a bunch of miniature plastic trees onto an old tea tray. She had made vines out of strips of green plastic cut from a garbage bag. When she took a shower, she brought the rainforest in with her.

On the back porch was the catapult she had made out of a plastic cup, a broken piece of hockey stick and a rubber band. She used it to toss peanuts at the squirrels.

Renata scratched her head. Scratching her head helped her think. All these other projects were small. Maybe it was time for something bigger. And then she remembered the refrigerator box.

Her parents had bought a new refrigerator. She had a hard time understanding why a new refrigerator got them so excited. "Look!" her dad had said. "It makes ice cubes!" "Amazing," her mom had sung. "It keeps lettuce crisp!" What interested Renata was the big cardboard box that the refrigerator had come in. She had asked her parents not to throw it out.

The box was in the basement. Renata went down and then pushed it up the stairs. On the side was the name of the refrigerator brand, Super Cool. Getting through doorways wasn't easy, but at last she pushed it into the middle of the living room. Of course she had to move

aside the coffee table and a bunch of
other stuff.

She lay down beside the box. Lying
down was also good for helping her think.

I know! she thought. A submarine!

A submarine like the ones that marine
biologists used to study the ocean. The
box was definitely big enough.

First of all, she needed a porthole to be able to see out. A porthole was a round window. But where would she find one of those? Then Renata remembered that the popcorn popper had a clear plastic dome on it. After you made popcorn, you could use the plastic dome as a bowl. Perfect!

She went into the kitchen to get the dome and then looked in a drawer for a pair of scissors. It wasn't easy to cut a hole in the box; she had to stick one point of the scissors through the thick cardboard and then use it like a saw, moving slowly around in a circle. Then she put the bowl over the hole and stuck down the edges with good old duct tape. She crawled into the box. Yup, she now had a nice porthole to look out.

Next up: a control panel.

In her closet, Renata kept a plastic bucket of discarded stuff—old switches and dials and buttons; the insides of broken radios and electronic games. She dragged the bucket inside the box and used glue and tape to make a control panel on one side. She thought it looked pretty good. She went back to her closet and found the screen of a toy television and taped it on the wall across from the control panel.

Hmm, thought Renata. Close.

But something was missing. Once more she went to her closet, but this

time she came out with a plastic steering wheel. The wheel had once belonged to a dump truck that was big enough to sit on. She wasn't sure if submarines had steering wheels, but she couldn't think of anything else to make it go where she wanted.

Something was still missing. Of course—a propeller! She went into the

kitchen and got two big wooden spoons
from a drawer. She lined them up
facing in opposite directions and taped
them together. Then she attached it to
the back.

Renata sat inside the box. "Not bad,"
she said. "Not bad at all." In fact, it
looked so good that she almost wished
she could show it to someone. But of

course that would mean having a friend over, and a friend was nothing but a pain in the neck. By herself, she could do whatever she wanted with it. And what she wanted to do was sit in the box and read another book on undersea life.

Ding-dong! Ding-dong!

The doorbell rang. Renata hated to be interrupted when she was working. Besides, she wasn't supposed to open the door to strangers. She ignored it.

Ding-dong! Ding-dong! Ding-dong!

Such an annoying sound! She crawled backward out of the box and went to the front window. She peeked through the curtains.

Oh no, she thought. Not Livingston Flott! He was going to spoil everything.

CHAPTER 3

The Right Thing

"Let me in! Let me in!"

Livingston Flott banged his fist on the door. He rang the doorbell again.

Renata opened the mail slot to speak through it. "Stop ringing the doorbell! And then go away!"

"You *have* to let me in," cried

Livingston. "My big brother's after me!"

"What did you do?"

"We were playing catch with his new baseball. I threw the ball and it went under your house. Then I couldn't get it out. And now he wants revenge. He says he's going to smash my guitar. You have to open up!"

Renata growled. This was exactly why she was glad to be an only child. No brothers or sisters to mess everything up. She couldn't just leave him there, so she opened the door. Livingston rushed in, locking the door behind him. He panted as he caught his breath. His guitar was hanging from a strap around his shoulder. It was plastic and had only four strings.

"How long are you planning to stay?" Renata asked. She hoped he would say five minutes.

"Just an hour or two. By then my brother will have stopped looking for me. Thanks a lot, Wolfie, you saved my life."

"Wolfie?"

"That's what kids at school call you. Actually, they call you the Lone Wolf. Because you stay by yourself at recess. But I think Wolfie is nicer. Do you like it?"

Renata mulled it over. She had never had a nickname before, probably because she didn't have any friends. She couldn't decide if she liked it or not.

"At school everybody calls you Fly," she said.

"I know. Because I buzz around and annoy people. But I like to look at it in a positive way. I mean, a fly is persistent. A fly is a survivor. You can call me Fly if you say it in a nice way."

Renata didn't plan to call him anything. She wanted him to go home. She saw him shift his guitar from his shoulder to his hands. "What are you doing?" she asked.

"I'm going to do something to thank you for saving me. I'm going to make up a song for you. Making up songs is my specialty. I'm a genius at it. I've already made up about a zillion."

"I don't want a song."

"Here goes." Livingston began to strum his guitar and sing.

Wolfie, oh Wolfie,
*   you did the right thing.*
You opened the door and you
*   let me run in.*
'Cause I was being chased by one of
*   my kin*
Who was going to poke me with a stick
*   or a pin.*
And with a big brother you never
*   can win.*
So I came to your door and made
*   a big din . . .*

"That's enough, thank you very much," Renata said. "Can you go on like that forever?"

"Pretty much."

Renata looked at Livingston. He was short and chubby. He had weird hair that stuck out in all directions. He waved his hands all over the place and never stopped talking.

"Are you sure you can't go now?" she asked.

"If I even step outside, my brother will see me. He'll turn me into chopped liver."

"You could go to a friend's house."

Livingston nodded. "True. And I've got lots of friends. It's just that they're really busy. And they never answer their phones. So I don't see them too much. Actually, never."

Livingston took a step past her into the living room.

"Don't go in there!" she said. But it was too late.

"Is that a refrigerator box?"

"No."

"It *is*! You're so lucky! Did you put that porthole in it? What is it supposed to be, a submarine?"

"Maybe."

"Neat! Do you have a control panel inside?"

"Of course I do."

"Let me see."

"Okay, but don't touch anything."

He crawled through the back flaps of

the box. "Sweet!" came his muffled
voice. "You really know what you're
doing."

"Okay, come out now."

Livingston crawled out backward. He
stood up. "It's almost perfect, Wolfie,"
he said.

"What do you mean, 'almost'?"

"You've got a propeller, sure. But you could use some boosters."

"Boosters?"

"Sure. Have you got any toilet paper rolls?"

"I have some in my paper-craft bin."

"Bring them here. All of them. And some glue."

Renata bit her lip. She had never allowed people to interfere with her projects. On the other hand, boosters did sound like a good idea. She decided that he could help her attach the boosters and then go home.

She fetched the toilet paper rolls and together they stuck them along the bottom edge of the box. They looked like a row of mini-rockets. Renata had to admit they were a good addition.

"Thanks. You probably want to go home now, right?" she asked.

"Have you got any food supplies?" he asked.

"Food supplies?"

"Sure. Exploring the ocean is going to make a person hungry."

Renata scratched her head. It probably *was* a good idea to bring some food. So she went into the kitchen, with Livingston following behind. She got out her school lunch box and put in a juice box.

Livingston added a second juice box.

She put in an apple.

Livingston put in a second apple.

Whatever she put in—a packet of trail mix, a cookie—he doubled it. She didn't say anything but just went back to the living room and put the lunch box into the sub.

"What about unforeseen events?" he asked.

"Unforeseen events?"

"You know, things you don't expect. You need some extra equipment with you. Better safe than sorry."

Renata gave him a look. But she went into her room and came back carrying a plastic bin. "There's all kinds of junk in here," she said.

"Perfect. Put it in."

She slid it into the box.

"Great," he said, nodding hard. "So when are we leaving?"

"What do you mean, *we*?"

CHAPTER 4

Do You See What I See?

"Aw, come on, Wolfie," pleaded Livingston. "Didn't I help? Why, this thing would sink to the bottom without me. Now it'll really move through the ocean."

"I don't know what you're talking about. It's a cardboard box. It's not actually in the ocean."

"Sure, I know that. It's just pretending."

"I don't pretend, *Fly*," she said, using his nickname for the first time. "This is for *educational* purposes, not make-believe."

"But pretending is fun. You mean that you never do it?"

"I don't even know how. It's for kids."

"We *are* kids. Besides, would you really send me back out there when my brother's still mad about his baseball? Let me stay a little longer and I'll show you how to pretend. You might like it."

How had this happened? Renata had been looking forward to a nice long stretch of time by herself. And here she was dealing with Livingston Flott. Still, it couldn't hurt to try just once.

Then she would send him home.

"Okay, fine," she said. "What do we do?"

"First of all, we make you the captain." Livingston saluted. "Permission to board the Submarine Super Cool, captain?"

"The Submarine Super Cool? We never agreed to call it that."

"But the words are right on the side. See?"

Livingston took a black marker out of his pocket. He went over to the box and above the words Super Cool he wrote "Submarine" in crooked letters.

Renata sighed. "Oh all right. I'll go in first." She got down on her knees and crawled inside, with Livingston coming up behind her. She sat with her legs crossed. Being near the front, Renata was sitting at the steering wheel while Livingston sat next to the control panel.

"Now give me an order," he said.

"Um, let me think. Okay, check the old radio dial."

"You mean the pressure gauge?"

"Fine, the pressure gauge."

"Pressure normal," Livingston said.

"And the one next to it."

"Oxygen tanks full."

This pretending still felt kind of silly to Renata. What should she say next? She scratched her head. "Since this is the first run, we want to go easy on the sub. We'll head out from shore and go twenty feet down, make a circle and come back."

"Aye aye, captain."

"Main engines on."

Livingston snapped a switch. "Main engines on!"

Renata heard a low rumble. That was strange, she thought. Maybe someone outside was starting up a lawn mower.

The rumble got louder.

The box began to tremble.

"Fly, stop shaking us."

"I'm not. I thought you were doing it."

"You're so fidgety, you don't even know when you're bouncing up and down! Now what's that sound?"

Renata could hear a gurgling noise and then a sort of rush. She leaned toward the porthole and stared. Water was pouring into the house through the open windows! How could that be?

"Uh, Fly, would you look out there and tell me what you see."

"Sure." He peered out the porthole. "I see water gushing into your house. Cool!"

"Cool? My parents aren't going to think so! Look, the water is rising over the porthole! Are we leaking anywhere?"

"Negative, captain. We seem to be in

ship-shape. May I suggest we start the propeller?"

"I don't see why not."

"Propeller on!"

Livingston pressed a button. There was a sort of whirr and then the cardboard box began to move through the water. When Renata next looked out the porthole, she saw their coffee table float by. The water was rising quickly.

"We're going to smash into the ceiling!" Fly said. "You better steer this thing."

Renata was going to say that the steering wheel didn't really work. But instead she grabbed it and turned it to the left, aiming the box, or the submarine, or whatever it was, toward the open window. They did move left! Was the window big enough for them to pass through? As they moved forward, she could hear them bang into one side of the window. But a moment later they were through. Renata looked through the porthole again.

She saw a school of silver fish swim by.

They were being followed by a squid. A big squid.

"Fly," she said in a hushed voice. "Do you see what I see?"

"Man, do I ever, Wolfie. A pretty nice view of the ocean."

CHAPTER 5

Something Out There

"Nice view?" Renata looked at Livingston. "You really don't think this is weird? We were making a *pretend* submarine. How can a refrigerator box travel underwater?"

"How do I know? It's not like this has ever happened to me before, either. But I say we should just go with it."

"But this isn't logical," Renata protested. "It doesn't make sense."

"Who cares if it's logical? It's fun! Look outside, Wolfie. It's amazing."

Renata leaned toward the porthole and together they gazed out. "Hey," she said, "a clown fish!"

She and Livingston watched as the orange- and white-striped fish darted back and forth. "It's so beautiful," said Renata. "They live among poisonous sea anemones. The poison doesn't affect them. Isn't that cool?"

"This is such a special moment," Livingston said. "I feel a song coming on."

"Please don't, Fly."

But he was already strumming his guitar.

I think the ocean is really swell
Even if no one can hear you yell.
This is the place where lobsters dwell,
And what they're thinking,
  I sure can't tell . . .

"Uh, that's great, Fly, really," Renata said. "But maybe you should go easy on our oxygen supply."

"True. How about we have a snack? Ocean travel makes me hungry." He picked up the lunch box and opened it. "Cookie?"

"No thanks."

Livingston took a bite. "Are you sure?" he mumbled. "It's good."

"All right, then. Pass me one."

Livingston took out the other cookie

and held it like a Frisbee. He threw it toward her and she just managed to catch it. Renata took a bite. Livingston was right, exploring the ocean did make a person hungry. Just then something bonked her on the head.

"Ow!"

It was a juice box.

"Sorry, Wolfie. I thought you were looking. I bet we're the first kids ever to eat cookies in a submarine."

"Especially one they built themselves." They ate their cookies and sucked on the bent straws. Just as she finished, Renata saw something through the porthole. She wasn't close enough to see well so she nudged the submarine forward.

"There's something out there. You better come and look. It's white and round. What is it?"

Livingston came over. They waited for whatever it was to come into better view. "Unbelievable," Livingston said. "That's my brother's baseball!"

CHAPTER 6

Taking a Swim

Renata and Livingston watched the baseball as it floated along. It was going in the same direction as them at the same speed.

"But how did it get in the ocean?" Renata asked.

"Well, it was stuck under the house." Livingston shrugged. "Maybe the water dislodged it. This is a great chance."

"A chance for what?"

"A chance to get the baseball back, of course. Then I can give it to my brother. It'll save my life."

Renata shook her head. "The baseball is out there. And we're in here. How do you propose we get it?"

"Simple," Livingston said. "You take a little swim."

"Me?"

"You want to see what the ocean is like, don't you?"

"I'm pretty sure you need oxygen tanks to stay underwater."

"We can fix some up. There must be something in that plastic bin of stuff. Let me check."

Livingston pushed himself over to the bin. He began tossing things out—a Ping-Pong paddle, a cowboy hat, a hand puppet, swim fins. "Hmm, none

of these things are right. Wait a minute, what about the bin itself?"

He dumped everything out and turned the bin upside down. "It's even clear so you can see through it. Just put this over your head."

"You've got to be kidding me."

"Hey, if a cardboard box can be a submarine, I don't see why a plastic bin won't work as a diving helmet. And while you're at it, you might as well put on these swim fins."

Renata had to admit that it did make a strange kind of sense. She put the bin over her head and then pulled on the swim fins. "Wait a second. What if I float too far away?"

"Good point." Livingston began digging in the pile of stuff. "Aha!" He pulled out a long plastic skipping rope. "Tie one end to your ankle. I'll hold onto the other end so that I can pull you back into the sub."

So Renata tied one end to herself, making sure the knot wouldn't come undone. "I have to go out through the back flaps of the box. You close them up again fast so the water doesn't come in."

"Will do, Captain Wolfie. Might I suggest you take one last thing with you?"

"What's that?"

From the pile Livingston took out a baseball glove. She nodded and slipped

it on her hand. Then she moved toward
the back of the box. She held up one
finger. Two fingers. Three fingers. Then
she pushed through the flaps and dove
into the water.

What was the ocean like? Cold and wet. Renata let herself float. Yes, she really could breathe in the junk-bin helmet.

Renata looked up. She couldn't see the surface, which meant that they were deep. Turning over, she saw something moving slowly along. She wondered if she ought to be scared, and then she saw what it was. A sea turtle! Slowly it moved its flippers like the oars of a rowboat, turning toward Renata and bobbing its head as if in greeting as it went past. Amazing!

She turned to see if Livingston was watching from the porthole. He was making faces at her and pointing. Oh right—she was supposed to get the baseball!

The baseball had floated farther away. Renata kicked with her fins and glided toward it. But something tugged at her, holding her back. It was the skipping rope. She had stretched it to the limit.

She reached out her hand with the glove on it as far as she could toward the baseball. Still she couldn't reach it. She stretched even farther, afraid the skipping rope would snap, but it was just enough for the ball to float right into the glove. She looked back at Livingston, who gave her a thumbs-up.

Still holding the ball, she let herself drift. After all, Renata loved to be alone and this was about as alone as a person could get. And it felt good, at least for a while. And then it didn't feel as good. In fact, it felt kind of sad. The ocean, Renata thought, is really, really big. Could she actually be feeling . . . lonely?

That feeling other people said they had all the time?

She turned to the porthole and was glad to see Livingston still there. She motioned for him to pull her in. The skipping rope yanked at her ankle, pulling her backward. She felt like a fish on a line. The flaps opened and one last yank pulled her inside. Livingston closed them again.

Renata pulled the bin off her head. She shook herself like a dog coming in from the rain.

"You did it!" cried Livingston. "You got the baseball. Way to go, Wolfie. But now you're dripping all over the place."

"I can't do much about that. I'll just have to drip dry." She took off the fins and untied the skipping rope and put everything back in the bin. Meanwhile, Livingston was looking out of the porthole again.

His eyes grew wide.

"Now what?" Renata asked.

CHAPTER 7

Flying Breakfast!

Renata joined Livingston at the porthole. Sure enough, there was something moving toward them.

Something big.

Something really, really big.

It was definitely another submarine, made of gleaming metal. But it was a submarine in the shape of what, exactly?

"Hey, Wolfie," said Livingston. "Does that look like a giant toaster to you?"

That's exactly what it looked like to Renata. All she could do was nod as she watched the giant toaster sub get closer.

"Do you think it's friendly?" Livingston asked nervously. "After all, everybody likes toast. How could a toaster sub not be friendly?"

"I hope you're right," Renata managed to say, "because it's coming directly at us."

At that moment a screechy sound came from somewhere inside their own cardboard submarine. Renata and Fly both turned toward the toy television screen.

Bright lines shot across the screen. The screeching got louder. And then an image appeared. It was the image of a face. It was round and bald and had a black patch over one eye, a scruffy beard and a three-cornered hat.

The awful screeching changed. It sounded like words coming from the face, but the words were impossible to understand.

"Archoo . . . vizzy . . . shooop . . ."

"What is that thing?" cried Livingston.

"It looks just like my Uncle Bob," said Renata. "Except my uncle doesn't have a beard or an eye patch."

"Is your uncle a pirate?" asked Livingston. "Because that's what he looks like to me. Only I never heard of a pirate in a submarine before."

"Attention," said the face on the screen. "I am Pirate Bob. I control this ocean and you are not welcome here. But you have something that I want. I will not destroy you if you give it to me."

Renata asked, "What do you want?"

"I search the ocean for treasure but I'm tired of gold and silver. You have something special. It is white and round."

"The baseball?"

"Exactly."

Renata wiped her forehead in relief. "Well, if that's all you want, you can have it. We'll throw it out to you."

"No we won't!" shouted Livingston.

"Yes we will!" Renata hissed at him.

"That's my brother's lucky baseball. He caught it at a real baseball game. I have to give it back to him."

"You would rather we have to fight that sub? It's a hundred times bigger than ours."

"I'm telling you, Wolfie, you don't know my brother. He's even scarier than that guy."

Renata sighed. This is exactly what happens, she thought, when you agree to play with somebody else. "Fine," she said out loud. "But don't blame me for what happens. Sorry, Mr. Pirate, but we're keeping the ball."

The most horrible screech yet came from the screen. "What! You defy me? You will regret this."

"Actually," said Renata, "I regret it already."

"Prepare for an attack!" cried the face. The face broke up and disappeared from the screen.

"Maybe he's bluffing," said Livingston. "I bet he just goes away."

They both turned to look out the porthole. All the lights on the toaster sub turned red.

"Do you want to bet?" Renata asked.

Two objects flew out of the top of the sub. They were tall and thin and square. They looked like . . . giant pieces of toast! And they were moving through the water right toward them.

"The S.S. Super Cool is under attack!" cried Livingston. "What should we do, captain?"

"How do I know? Hold onto something!"

The first piece of toast sailed right past them. But the corner of the second one banged against the box, sending it into a spin. *"Ahh!"* cried Livingston as he was thrown to the floor. *"Hit by breakfast food!"*

Renata grabbed the steering wheel and managed to hold on, although she got banged about. "I don't see any other way," she said. "We're just going to have to work together."

"You mean like a *team?*" Livingston clasped the edge of the control panel. "You mean like *friends?*"

"This is no time for a discussion. I'm going to point us toward the ocean surface. We've got to outrun that giant sub. When I say so, you hit the main engine and the toilet paper rolls—I mean the boosters—at the same time. If we can take him by surprise, I think we'll have a chance."

"You mean we should just run away?"

"That's exactly what I mean."

"Sounds good to me."

"On my count," Renata said. "One, two—"

"He's firing more toast!"

"THREE!"

Livingston hit buttons. He hit switches. He hit everything. There was a tremendous groan and roar as they shot forward and up. Both of them were thrown backward. Renata had to make her way back to the wheel.

The Submarine Super Cool powered up through the ocean, leaving the giant toaster sub behind.

CHAPTER 8

Floating Furniture

Renata and Livingston continued at
top speed, eager to get away from the
maniacal pirate with his deadly toast.
Renata held tight to the steering
wheel. How did she know the way
back to her own house? She didn't.

All she could do was head for the surface. She watched through the porthole as they passed a hammerhead shark and a giant jellyfish. Every so often she had to maneuver around pieces of junk that thoughtless humans had dumped into the ocean—an old DVD player, a sofa and even a toilet.

"People are such slobs," she said. "We make the ocean our garbage can."

"True enough, Wolfie," said Livingston. "Hey, my guitar wasn't hurt by all that bouncing around. I think this calls for a new song."

"That's really not necessary."

"It's no trouble at all." He began to strum.

He had a beard and an eye patch too,
And for all I know, he wore one shoe
And ate for his lunch a bowl of goo.
But our fearless captain knew what to do!
We hit the gas and away we flew . . .

"I hate to interrupt," said Renata, "but isn't that the surface above us?"

They looked out the porthole. Yes, there was the surface of the ocean with the sun glinting off it. To Renata, it was the most beautiful thing she'd ever seen.

"You know what they say about voyages," said Livingston. "It's good to go and it's good to come home again. That is, if we can find our way home. Hey, here's one switch I haven't tried. I wonder what it does."

"I don't think it's the time to find out."

But Livingston had already flicked the switch. A new sound began, a high-pitched whistle. They felt the sub surge forward at tremendous speed.

"*Yee-haw!*" cried Livingston.

"We're coming in too fast!" Renata said. "We'll fly right up out of the water and smash to bits. We have to do something. Reverse boosters!"

Livingston looked at the control panel. How did he do that? There were no more controls left unused. He took out his marker and over a button he wrote "Reverse." Then he pressed it.

This time the roar was more of a growl. The sub slowed down but it was still going pretty fast. Renata looked

out the porthole and saw something strange. It looked like furniture floating on the ocean surface. She could see the bottom of a sofa and chairs and even a coffee table. And it all looked familiar. Wait a minute! That was her living room! She turned the wheel a little to the left and aimed for the space between the sofa and the table.

"The sub is about to surface!" she cried. "Get ready!"

"How do I do that?" asked Livingston.

"Hold on!"

Renata held the steering wheel steady and closed her eyes.

CHAPTER 9

Lucky

Renata felt a smack as the cardboard sub hit the surface. Immediately it began to fly apart, sending her and Livingston tumbling.

Renata blinked her eyes. She pushed a piece of cardboard off of her and saw that she was sprawled on her own living room sofa. Across from her, Livingston was hanging upside down from the top of an easy chair. When she looked down, she saw an inch of water swirling over the floor.

The front door burst open.

"Renata! Renata! Are you all right? Speak to us!"

It was her mom and dad. "Oh,
darling," her mom cried, hurrying to
her side. "We heard on the radio in the
car that a pipe burst on our street and all
the houses got flooded. We rushed
home as fast as we could. You could
have been hurt."

"I was worried that those pipes were too old," her dad said. "But who's hanging upside down from the chair? Is that Livingston Flott?"

"Hi, Mr. Wolfman," Livingston said cheerfully. He let himself slip down and got right side up. "Wolfie—I mean Renata—asked me in to play."

"She did?" asked her mom. "Good for you, Renata. But the two of you must be in shock. What can we do after we mop up this mess to make you feel better?"

"Some ice cream might help," Livingston suggested.

It so happened that Renata's parents had picked up a tub of chocolate swirl ice cream on the way home. Her dad turned off the water and then they got out all the mops and rags and everyone helped to dry the floor. "Hey, look!" Livingston said, picking up a damp cushion. Underneath was his brother's baseball.

"You've got to be kidding," Renata said.

In the kitchen, her mom dished out two big bowls of ice cream and insisted that they eat up every last drop.

"That sure helps a lot," Livingston said, a ring of chocolate around his mouth. "I better get going. My parents will wonder where I am."

"Renata, it's so nice you've made a friend," said her mom. "Why don't you walk Livingston to the door."

"What for?"

"Because that's what friends do."

"Okay." Renata shrugged. She walked with Livingston to the door and then outside. They stood together on the porch.

"So tell me, Wolfie," Livingston said. "Are we?"

"Are we what?" she asked.

"Friends. Are we really friends?"

"I don't have friends," Renata insisted. "I don't need friends. I don't *want* friends."

"But you have to admit that it was fun today," Livingston said.

Renata scratched her head. "Yes, I admit that it was fun."

"So can I come over again?"

"I guess so."

"Cool! We'll be Wolfie and Fly. We'll have adventures together. When the two of us are together, who knows what will happen?"

"Okay. But we're still not friends."

"Right," Livingston agreed. "See you around, Wolfie."

"Bye, Fly."

Renata watched Livingston hop down the stairs. He turned around and made a funny face. Then he started to walk like a chimpanzee.

"You're a weirdo," she called. But she laughed anyway.

And he was right, she thought. When Wolfie and Fly are together, who knows what might happen?

ACKNOWLEDGEMENTS

First, a mighty big thanks to Tara Walker
and Samantha Swenson and the rest of the
gang at Tundra books. Also to Rebecca
Comay for first hearing about these two
oddballs, to my parents for giving us those
giant cardboard boxes to play with, and to all
the kids in the schools I've been privileged to
visit for their enthusiasm and feedback.

Look for

next adventure . . . coming soon!